Macca the Alpaca

MATT COSGROVE

For my mum, Nancy. Thank you for EVERYTHING — M.C

First published in 2017 by Koala Books
An imprint of Scholastic Australia Pty Limited

First published in the UK in 2019 by Scholastic Children's Books
Euston House, 24 Eversholt Street
London NW1 1DB
A division of Scholastic Ltd
www.scholastic.co.uk
London ~ New York ~ Toronto ~ Sydney ~ Auckland
Mexico City ~ New Delhi ~ Hong Kong

ISBN 978 1407 19361 8

1 3 5 7 9 10 8 6 4 2

Typeset in Mr Dodo featuring Festivo LC.

This guy is called **Macca.**

He's an alpaca!

He loves **splashing** in puddles and gives

the **best**
cuddles!

Macca's days were carefree, filled with **giggles** and **glee** until..· DRAMA!

A llama.

That guy is called **Harmer,**
(not your average charmer).

He's **tall, STRONG** and **woolly,**

but also a ...

Harmer was mean,

quite the **worst** you have seen!

He took Macca's stuff and played very **rough.**

'You **PUNY** *pipsqueak,*

I'm **STRONG** and you're *weak!*'

Macca said,

'No, you're wrong,
I'm **surprisingly**
strong.'

The pair made a bet and
a **challenge was set.**

'I'll move this boulder!'   Harmer pushed with his shoulder.

He **huffed, puffed** and **nudged** 'til it finally budged.

When Macca's turn came,
he just **used his brain.**

Hmph!

'Well, why don't you try to reach up this high?!'

'Easy done,
using this.'

Harmer
let out a
hiss.

Now that llama was **FUMING!**

His nasty mind *zooming.*

'Okay, let's have a **race!**
Try and keep pace.
First to the top is the best . . .

full stop.'

They took off in a flash
and began their **mad dash**
up the steep mountain side.

But then . . .

the rocks

started to

slide.

Being **nimble** and **light**,
Macca made it alright.
As he leapt to the summit,
he saw Harmer PLUMMET!

Some might call it karma,
as that bully of a llama

went . . .

CRASH,

BANG

and

SPLAT!

And that, my friends,
was that.

Harmer said, plainly **shaken**,

'Turns out I was mistaken,
for you've proved it quite clearly,
size doesn't matter, really.'

Macca went up to the thug
and gave him

a **great,**
big...